Mr S. G. Pothan worked for the Indian Railways for more than forty years. He published four children story books.

Shobita Punja has worked in the field of education for more than fifteen years, training teachers and preparing educational material. She now writes books on Indian Art and History.

Other Children's Books by Shobita Punja

Listen to the Animals

STORIES ABOUT THIS AND THAT

Shobita Punja

*(As told to her by
her grandfather, S.G. Pothan)*

Illustrations by

Mario de Miranda

PUFFIN BOOKS

Penguin Books India (P) Ltd., 210, Chiranjiv Tower, 43, Nehru Place,
New Delhi 110 019, India
Penguin Books Ltd., 27 Wrights Lane, London W8 5TZ, UK
Penguin Books USA Inc., 375 Hudson Street, New York,
New York 10014, USA
Penguin Books Australia Ltd., Ringwood, Victoria, Australia
Penguin Books Canada Ltd., 10 Alcorn Avenue, Suite 300, Toronto, Ontario M
3B2, Canada
Penguin Books (NZ) Ltd., 182-190 Wairau Road, Auckland 10, New Zealand

First published by Penguin Books India (P) Ltd. 1994

Copyright © Shobita Punja 1994

10 9 8 7 6 5 4 3 2 1

All rights reserved

Typeset in Palatino by Gulmohur Press, New Delhi

To my grandfather,
S. G. Pothan
and
Rebecca, my grandmother

Dear Friend,

The stories in this book were all written or told to me by my grandfather, S. G. Pothan. When I was a little girl he used to let me sit on his lap and he would tell me stories. They were stories about animals and people, about this and that and from here and there. The stories were about kindness and friendship, how people are and how we should behave.

You can read these stories out aloud. You can ask your parents, grandparents, elder brother or sister, to read them to you. You can make the stories into plays or puppet shows in your school. You can write stories of your own.

The beautiful pictures in this book were drawn nearly thirty years ago by Mario de Miranda. He is a famous artist of India and has illustrated many books. I am very grateful to him for allowing me to use his pictures for this book. I hope after reading these stories you will make your own drawings.

I loved my grandfather very much and I have always loved his stories. I wish that you too could hear him tell them. I have rewritten those that I love the most and offer them to you as a gift from my grandfather.

Shobita Punja

12 October 1993
New Delhi

Dear Tanya,

The stories in this book were all told to me
by my grandfather S.G. Indran. Indra was a little
girl he used to listen to on his lap and he would tell
her stories. They were stories about animals and people,
about hills and their journeys, much more. The stories
were about kindness and friendship, how people are
and how we should behave.

You can read these stories out aloud. You can ask
your parents, grandparents, elder brother or sister to
read them to you. You can make the stories into plays
or puppet shows at your school. You can take the stories
on your own.

The beautiful pictures in this book were drawn
nearly thirty years ago by Mario de Miranda. He is a
famous artist of India and has illustrated many books.
I am very grateful to him for allowing me to use his
pictures for this book. I hope that while reading the stories
you will make your own drawings.

I loved my grandfather very much and I have always
loved his stories. I wish that you too could hear him
tell them. I have rewritten those that I love the most
and offer them to you as a gift from my grandfather.

Sheena Puri

12 October 1997
New Delhi

CONTENTS

1

WHO IS THE GREATEST OF US ALL?

There was once a king who was very proud. He thought he was the greatest king on earth. No one could say anything to him that he did not like. Everyone had to say what the king liked to hear. Whenever the king sent out a new order his people would obey it. The people trembled and feared their proud king.

One day, the king sent out an order that every man should bring his eldest daughter to the royal court so that he could choose the prettiest girl to be his wife.

In this country there lived a poor but honest man who was only a humble sweeper. He was very wise and helpful and his neighbours loved him very much. He was the only man in the whole kingdom who did not fear the king.

He would always tell his friends, 'I work hard all day. I try to be good. I try not to hurt anyone. Why should I be frightened of the king? Why should I obey the king's orders which I know are wrong?'

The sweeper had only one daughter who was very beautiful. She was also a hard-working girl and had grown up to be polite and kind. The sweeper was very fond of his daughter not only because she was beautiful but also because she was kind and gentle.

The sweeper wanted his daughter to marry the village rat-catcher. He was a handsome and funny man. The rat-catcher was a helpful sort of person who helped everyone in the village to catch rats that were eating up their food, stores, and clothes.

The sweeper was very angry when he heard that the king had ordered everyone to bring their daughters to the royal court so that he could choose a wife. He knew the king's order was stupid, foolish and very wrong. The old sweeper made up his mind that he would not obey the king even if it cost him his life.

The next day, every father in the kingdom went with his eldest daughter to the king's court. The sweeper went too, but he did not take his daughter.

The day passed peacefully and the king met many pretty girls. When the sweeper's turn came he stood in front of the king, without his daughter.

The king flew into a mighty rage when he saw the sweeper without his daughter. He said, 'I shall cut off your head for disobeying my order.'

The sweeper was not afraid and in a quiet voice said, 'Your Majesty! I am a poor sweeper. I sweep the streets which everyone makes dirty. No one else cleans the streets because everyone thinks that sweeping is a lowly job. But I believe that the rat-catcher does not look down on me. He likes me and I like him. I think the rat-catcher is the greatest man. I would be happy if my daughter wished to marry the rat-catcher.'

'What? You think that the rat-catcher is greater than a king. Do you think the rat-catcher is greater than me?' roared the king.

'Yes, Your Majesty! I think the rat-catcher is the best and greatest man in the whole world and I would like my daughter to marry him.'

The king was very, very angry. He shouted, 'Off with his head! Kill this man just now.'

As the king's guards came running up to the sweeper, the king said, 'Wait a minute!'

There was silence in the court. Everyone was listening to the king. If a tiny pin had fallen on the ground, you would have heard it.

The king looked at the brave and fearless sweeper and asked, 'Before my guards cut off your head, tell me something. Why do you think the rat-catcher is the greatest man in the kingdom?'

The sweeper said, 'Your Majesty, what do you think is the most powerful thing in the world?'

The king said, 'The sun. It rises every morning and crosses the sky, never too fast, never too slow. In the light and warmth of the sun, everything grows. Without the sun there would be no seasons, no plants, no animals, no human beings. There would be nothing on earth without the sun.'

The sweeper said, 'Your Majesty, I work outdoors all day long in the hot sun cleaning the roads and the streets. I have watched the sun and its movements across the sky, each day. One day, I asked the sun if it was the greatest.

'The sun said, "It is not I who is the greatest thing in the world. The clouds are greater than me. The clouds can hide my face and make me disappear. The clouds can make a hot day cool, they can drive away the heat and bring rain. Surely the clouds are greater than the sun!" '

The sweeper paused and said, 'So I asked a cloud which was flying in the sky if it was the greatest in the world?

'The cloud replied, "It is not I. The wind is greater than a cloud. The wind can blow a cloud away, the wind can carry the clouds across the sky. A cloud cannot move without the wind."

'So I asked the wind if it was the greatest of all things.

'The wind said, "It is not I. Though I can blow the clouds across the sky. I can bend the branches of the trees. When I am funny, I can blow your hair and make it a mess. When gentle, I can blow out a candle. I can fan you with a cool breeze. I can carry sweet perfumes across the land. When I am angry I can blow the roofs off the houses. I can destroy whole cities. But alas, I cannot move a mountain." '

The king was listening very quietly to the story. Everyone in the royal court was listening to the sweeper's story.

The sweeper went on, 'Then I went to the mountain and told it that it must be the greatest of us all.

5

'The mountain replied, "I am great but not the greatest. I am tall and strong. The wind cannot move me. I am bigger than houses, taller than trees, heavier than a thousand fat men. But I cannot stop the little brown rat from burrowing its hole in me. I am great but I am not the greatest. The rat is greater than me!"

'Then I found a brown rat, Your Majesty!' said the sweeper. 'I asked the rat who was the greatest.

'The rat replied, "I am great but not the greatest. There is a rat-catcher in the village and I am very frightened of him." '

The old sweeper bowed low before the king and said, 'So you see, Your Majesty, though the rat-catcher is poor and humble and no one likes his work yet in some ways he is the greatest!'

The king and all the people were struck with wonder at what the wise sweeper had said.

Turning to the sweeper the king said, 'Dear man, you shall not die, but if you wish you shall be my minister. I like you because you are not afraid to speak the truth. You are not afraid of anyone. You are wise and you are kind. Please help me rule this kingdom and make my people happy.'

2

THE CROCODILE AND THE JACKAL PLAY

There was a crocodile who lived in a pond near the village. He was very big, with four short legs and a very long tail. The crocodile had a very big mouth and when he opened it, you could see two long rows of sharp white teeth. Whenever anyone came to the pond he would try to catch them. He would catch their legs in his mouth and drag them into the water and then eat them up. Everyone in the village was frightened of the crocodile.

One year there was no rain. There was very little water in the pond. The crocodile was left on the hot, dry sand. Crocodiles have to live in water. They like to come up and sun themselves on the sand but when they get too hot, they slip into the water and cool down. Without water to cool down crocodiles can die of the heat.

Soon the pond dried up and the crocodile was very worried. When anyone passed by, the crocodile would shout out, 'Please, save me! I am being roasted to death in the heat.'

Everyone saw the crocodile and heard his shouts. But no one wanted to help him. Everyone was frightened of the crocodile. Some people answered the crocodile's cries and said, 'Serves you right! You always trouble us, why should we take the trouble to help you?'

One day, an old man was passing the pond. He saw the sad and dying crocodile and said, 'I will show you a pond which never goes dry and is always full of fresh water.'

The crocodile was very weak as he had not eaten for days. However, he followed the old man. They walked and walked till they came to a pond full of water.

The old man got into the water and said, 'Look, the water in this pond is very deep. When I stand in the water it comes up to my neck. Come in and enjoy yourself in the pond.'

The crocodile slowly slipped into the water. Then he swam in the pond for a little while till he was nice and cool. Then diving into the water he grabbed the old man's leg. 'Hey! What are you doing? That is my leg!' screamed the old man.

'Yes, I know it is your leg,' said the crocodile. 'But it is a long time since I ate anything. I am going to eat you up, old man.'

'How can you do that!' cried the old man. 'I helped you find this pond. I saved your life. Now you want to eat me. What an ungrateful creature you are!'

Just then a jackal came to the pond to drink some water. He heard the crocodile and the old man talking and shouted, 'What is the matter?'

The old man with his leg still in the crocodile's mouth said, 'Let us ask the jackal. If he says that you are right, then you can eat me.'

The old man called the jackal and told him the story. He told him how he had saved the crocodile.

9

How they had walked together and found this pond full of water. Then he asked, 'Do you think the crocodile should eat me after all the help I have given him?'

The jackal thought for a while. He drank a little water and thought a bit more. Then the jackal said, 'How can I say anything? I have not seen the pond where the crocodile used to live.'

So the crocodile and the old man got out of the water. The crocodile, the old man and the jackal walked all the way back to the dried up pond.

The jackal said, 'Now show me where you found the crocodile.'

The crocodile went and lay in exactly the same spot on the hot, dry sand.

The jackal whispered to the old man, 'Quick, run away! You are a foolish fellow to help the crocodile. Run! This is your chance. You run one way and I will run the other way.'

The poor crocodile could do nothing. He was very angry with the jackal. The crocodile decided that one day he would punish the jackal for playing this trick.

Soon after this it began to rain and the pond was filled with clean water once again. The crocodile knew that the jackal would come to the pond to drink water and decided to catch him then and eat him up. So he lay in wait day after day.

One day, the jackal came to the pond and bent his head and drank some water. The crocodile swam under water very slowly and came near the jackal. Then the crocodile opened his mouth and caught the jackal's leg.

The jackal began to laugh and said, 'What a fool you are! You think you have caught my leg. You silly fellow, you have caught a root of the tree in your mouth.'

The crocodile believed the jackal and opened his mouth and the jackal ran away.

The crocodile was very, very angry with the jackal. He lay in the sand and thought of another plan. He knew that the jackal liked the fruit of the jamun tree. Near the pond was a tall, beautiful jamun tree. In the summer, the plums became ripe and began to fall to the ground. The crocodile pushed and rolled all the jamuns together and made a big heap. Then he crawled and hid beneath the heap of jamun plums. The jackal came to the pond and saw the heap of nice, juicy jamuns. He went near and looked at the ripe fruit. His mouth watered as he longed to eat the bitter-sweet fruit.

Just as he was going to take one fruit, he saw something shining. He knew that the shining object, under the heap of jamuns, were really the teeth of the crocodile. So he quickly jumped and ran away to a safe distance and said, 'You foolish crocodile, you can never catch me.'

The crocodile was not going to give up so easily and tried to catch the jackal again and again. Everytime he tried to catch the jackal, he failed because the jackal was quick and very lucky.

One day, the crocodile lay down on the sandy bank of the pond and pretended to be dead. He lay very still because he knew that the jackal would come when he saw a dead body. Soon the jackal came by. When he saw the body of the crocodile, he came nearer and nearer. The jackal sniffed the ground to find out if the crocodile was really dead. He felt the ground with his paws and noticed that the ground was still wet. He guessed that the crocodile must have come out of the water just a little while ago.

The jackal went closer to the crocodile. He said, 'The crocodile is dead. I can have a good meal tonight.' Then he went a little closer to the crocodile and said, 'If you are really dead, you will shake your toe.'

The crocodile wiggled his toe.

The jackal laughed and shouted, 'You cannot catch me with any of your tricks.'

Do you know something? The crocodile and the jackal are still playing tricks on each other.

3

SUNITA AND HER FRIENDS

There once lived a merchant who had a grown-up son called Rahul and a small daughter named Sunita. He was very fond of his two children. Their mother had died a long time ago. As he was a merchant he travelled far to different countries. While he was away on a journey, he died.

His son married Radha, the only daughter of a rich man. She was very beautiful, but very proud and jealous. Rahul hoped that Radha would look after Sunita. She did not like Sunita because everyone loved that sweet little girl.

Rahul did the same work as his father. He was a merchant and travelled to far-off countries. Whenever he was away, Sunita lived with her sister-in-law. Sunita used to work all day but Radha, her sister-in-law would give her very difficult jobs to do. When Sunita failed to do them, she was punished.

There was a pretty forest near the house. Whenever Sunita was sad and unhappy she would go to the forest and sit under a tree and cry. She would talk to the trees and birds and animals. She would water the trees and plants. She would feed the birds with grains of rice whenever she could.

Soon the animals and birds got used to Sunita and not one of them was afraid of her. They would eat the scraps that she brought and listen to her sad story. While she sat beneath the tree the animals and birds would play about and do their work. Soon they all became very fond of her. Sunita loved to go to the forest to be with her friends.

One day, Rahul said goodbye to Sunita and went on a long journey. He told his wife to look after Sunita. Radha promised to do so, but in her heart she was angry that everyone loved Sunita so much. Sunita was very sad on the day her brother left the house. She began to spend more and more time each day in the forest with her friends the birds and the animals.

One day, Sunita was going to the well to fetch some water. She looked at the pot and saw that there were three holes in the bottom. She told her sister-in-law that the pot had holes in it. Radha got angry and said, 'You are such a lazy girl. Go and fetch water from the well. Do not make excuses. Fetch the water quickly.'

Sunita knew she could not bring water in a pot with holes. She also knew that her sister-in-law would shout at her if she did not bring the water.

With tears in her eyes she took the pot and went to the forest. She sat beneath her favourite tree and began to cry. A little frog was hopping past her and heard her crying. 'What is the matter, sweet Sunita?' asked the frog.

Sunita told the frog that she could not fetch water in a pot with holes. Seeing her looking so

15

sad, the frog came nearer and said, 'Sunita, I feel very sorry for you. We know that your sister-in-law is not kind to you. You have been very kind to us. We want to help you. Do not worry! I will call two of my brothers. We like water. Do not worry about the holes.'

Sunita watched the frog. He called two other frogs and together they jumped into the pot. Each frog pressed himself against one of the holes in the pot and closed it up. Sunita took the pot to the well and filled it up with water. She ran home as quickly as she could, without spilling even a drop of water. Her sister-in-law was surprised to see that Sunita had brought the water without spilling a drop. She could not get angry with Sunita.

A few days later, the cruel sister-in-law called Sunita and gave her a tiny piece of string. Radha told Sunita to go to the forest and fetch enough firewood for the kitchen. 'If you do not bring enough firewood I shall beat you, you lazy girl! Bring the firewood as quickly as you can. If you are slow, I will not be able to cook any lunch today and we will both go hungry.'

Sunita's eyes filled with tears. She ran to the forest and sat under her favourite tree. She did not know what to do. In a while she got up and began to pick up the dried and dead wood from the forest floor. Soon she had collected a big pile of dead wood. Then she tried to tie up the bundle of wood with the tiny piece of string. The string was too short and she could not tie the twigs together. 'What am I going to do? I cannot tie the bundle. How will I carry the firewood home?'

As she was thinking, she saw a snake crawling near her. 'Mr Snake! Please tell me what to do. I do not have a long enough string to tie up this bundle of firewood. I have to take the bundle home. If I do not take the firewood home, my sister-in-law will shout and we will not have any food to eat.'

The snake came near her and said, 'Do not cry, Sunita! I shall help you. Gather the firewood and I will help you carry it back.'

Sunita obeyed and made a nice, fat bundle of wood. Then the snake came and said, 'I will stretch myself on the ground. Lay the sticks one by one in the middle of my body. When you have put as many as you can carry, I shall wind myself around the bundle like a rope. Then you can lift the bundle and carry the firewood safely on your head.'

Sunita thanked the snake. She carried the bundle on her head and walked home. When she reached her house, she put the bundle down on the ground. The snake unwound himself and quietly slipped away. Sunita called out to her sister-in-law. Radha was very surprised to see the big bundle of firewood without a piece of string. She was very angry but she could not find an excuse to shout at Sunita.

One day, the sister-in-law was working in the kitchen. She had spread the rice on a big cloth and left it to dry in the sun. Then she went to the storeroom to get a pot of wheat to grind. The pot of wheat fell from her hands and broke. All the wheat fell on top of the rice grains. She tried to pick up the pieces of the broken pot but while she was doing this the wheat got mixed up with the rice. Radha got angry with herself. She knew that she would not be able to separate the rice from the wheat.

Just then Sunita walked past the kitchen. Radha said to her, 'Sunita, come here. I do not know who has mixed the rice and wheat together. I want you to separate the grains of wheat and rice quickly. Otherwise there will be no food for either of us today.'

Sunita looked at the mixture with horror. She did not know what to do. She carried the bundle of grain to the forest and sat under her favourite tree. She began to work. She worked hard but she knew that she would never be able to finish the task. She started crying in despair.

There were many sparrows sitting on the tree and on the ground in front of Sunita. They heard her crying and asked her what the matter was. On hearing the story, the sparrows said, 'Do not worry. We will help you. We can pick up even the smallest grain with our beaks. We will do the task in a short time.'

The flock of sparrows set to work at once. Soon the rice was separated from the wheat. Sunita ran into the house and got two trays and put the rice in one and the wheat in the other. She carried the trays back to the house and showed them to her sister-in-law.

Some days later Radha fell ill. Her face became red and horrid. Radha was very angry that she did not look beautiful anymore. She called Sunita and said, 'Take this pot and go to the seashore. I want you to collect some foam from the sea. I need the foam to put on my face. Then I will get better and I will be able to cook and look after you. If you do not get the sea foam, I will surely die.'

Sunita took the pot and went to the seashore. Each time the waves came in, she saw the lovely white foam riding on the crest of the wave. Each time she went to the wave and tried to pick up the foam, it disappeared. And though she spent the day trying to collect foam, it would turn into sea-water each time she touched it.

By the evening, Sunita had not been able to collect any foam. She was very tired and knew that she could not do anything. She sat on the shore and looked at the sea. She saw a large ship sailing towards the shore. There were many people waiting on the beach for the ship. Sunita got up and walked towards the crowd. She watched the ship come in. She watched the people get out of the ship and come to the shore. In the crowd she recognized one person. He saw her too.

Sunita was overjoyed because her brother Rahul had returned home at last. Sunita was really happy.

Rahul hugged Sunita and picked her up and asked, 'How are you, my little sister? Did you miss me?' As he said that, big tears began to roll down Sunita's cheeks. She cried and cried and hugged her brother.

'What is the matter, little sister?' asked Rahul.

Then Sunita told him the whole story about the difficult things that she had had to do. Rahul was very angry.

Sunita and Rahul returned home. He did not give his wife any of the presents that he had brought for her. He told Radha that she had been very cruel and unkind to Sunita.

He gave Sunita lots of presents and then asked, 'What can I do to make you happy?'

Sunita replied, 'I want you to promise me that you will never spoil the forest that we have near our house. I want your permission to go to the forest every day and feed the birds and animals and to water the trees. You see, brother, all my friends live in that forest!'

4

TWO SISTERS

In a distant village there lived two sisters. The name of the eldest sister was Leela and the younger sister's name was Lula. The sisters used to play together in the forest near their home every day. They would climb the trees and play hide-and-seek. They would splash and swim in the river. The two sisters loved playing together.

One day, Lula said to her sister, 'Let us go and visit our old uncle who lives across the stream.'

Leela frowned and said, 'You go. I am not going to walk so far in the hot sun just to see an old uncle.'

Lula made up her mind to go and see her uncle across the stream. When she told her parents they were very happy. Her grandmother made some delicious cakes for her to take on her trip and said, 'One cake is for you and two of these cakes are for your uncle.'

Lula set out early in the morning. It was a lovely day. The sun was warm and the forest looked beautiful. Lula began to sing and skip along the path through the forest. She saw her favourite mango tree. She looked again and noticed that one large branch was broken and hanging down. The whole tree was bending with the weight of the broken branch. Seeing it Lula said, 'Oh dear! You must be in such pain with the weight of such a heavy branch dragging you down. Let me see if I can help you.' Lula pulled off the broken branch and the tree was able to stand straight again.

Further ahead, Lula saw a fire. She looked around but could not see who had made the fire. The fire was still burning and little flames were spreading, eating up the dead leaves and twigs around it. Lula stopped and put her packet of cakes on the ground. She looked around for some small stones. She made a ring of stones around the fire so that it would not spread and burn the forest. She then stoked the fire and removed the ash. Soon the fire began burning brightly. When Lula saw that everything was safe she set off again.

Lula walked till she came to the small stream. Her uncle lived on the other side. The stream was very pretty. The water was always clean and fresh. Many birds and animals came to drink its water. There were tall bamboos and grasses growing on either side of the stream. Lula decided that she would sit beside the stream for a little while. She would play a little in the water before she crossed the stream to visit her uncle on the other side.

When she came to the stream she saw that the water was blocked with stones and sand. She could not hear the pretty gurgling sound that the stream made as it splashed against the rocks. 'Oh poor thing! I am sure you are very unhappy since you cannot run, laugh or gurgle over the rocks and stones.' Saying this Lula carefully picked up the stones and removed the sand. Soon the little stream began to flow along cheerfully. The clear

24

water ran over the stones and rocks gurgling and laughing all the way.

At long last Lula crossed the stream and reached her uncle's house. She ran up and hugged him and said, 'Uncle, I am so happy to see you. How are you? I have brought some cakes for you. Let us sit together and eat them.'

Lula's uncle was very happy to see her. He thanked her for coming to visit him and for bringing the cakes.

They spent the day together laughing and talking. When it was time to go Lula's uncle said, 'Before you go, there is something I wish to give you.'

He went inside the house and opened his cupboard. He took out a beautiful gold coin and gave it to Lula. 'I do not have much to give you. I want to give you something that will remind you of me. Keep this coin carefully. I give it with all my love.'

Lula was very happy and pressed the coin against her lips and kissed it. She hugged her uncle and promised him that she would be back soon.

All the way back she sang happily to herself. She came to the stream and watched it flowing by. Looking upstream she saw a beautiful silk scarf floating on the water. 'Take the scarf, Lula. I have carried the scarf on my breast just for you!' the stream seemed to say to Lula. Lula got into the water and picked up the scarf and thanked the stream for its kindness.

She walked along waving her new scarf and singing happily to herself. Soon she got a little tired and wanted to sit down and rest. She saw in the distance the little fire that she had looked after. She went and sat near it. The fire was nice and warm. Lula sat beside it for a while. On the ring of stones that she had put around the fire was a warm glass of milk. 'Someone has left this for me to drink,' she thought. She drank the milk and thanked the fire and went on her way.

She had not gone very far when she saw her favourite mango tree. She looked again and saw that there were many mangoes hanging hidden behind the branches. She climbed the tree and plucked some mangoes. She thanked the tree and said, 'I will take the mangoes as a present for my mother, father and sister.'

With her hands full of presents she went back home.

Her sister, Leela, saw her coming home and ran to greet her. When she saw all the lovely gifts that Lula had brought she was very jealous.

A few days later Leela told her mother that she too wanted to see her uncle who lived across the stream. She thought to herself, 'If I go to see my uncle I will also get many presents along the way.'

So, early next morning, Leela set out. Along the way she saw a mango tree. The tree cried out as she walked by, 'Leela, please stop and tidy up my branches.' This made Leela very angry and in a very loud voice she said, 'Who do you think I am? Do you think I am so silly as to waste my time looking after trees? Do what you have to do yourself!' Saying this she went on.

She too came to a small fire and found that it was smoking and coughing. Seeing Leela the fire said, 'Please, Leela, will you kindly clear away the ash and help me burn brightly? I am choking to death.'

'Do you think I have no other work but to dirty my hands removing the ash and stoking the fire? I cannot waste time. I am going to see my uncle and collect presents from him.'

She walked and walked until she came to the stream. The stream called out to Leela and said, 'Leela, please help me. The leaves and stones have made a dam across my water. Please move them away from me. So that I can run wild and free.'

27

'You are silly to get stuck like that. Clear it up yourself. I cannot get wet. I cannot help you.'

Wasting no time she rushed across the stream to her uncle's house. When she arrived at the house she found her uncle lying in bed. 'What is the matter?' asked Leela.

'I am very sick, my child. Can you stay a little while and look after me and talk to me?' said the uncle.

'Oh dear, I am in a bit of a hurry. I have to get home,' said Leela.

'Then you must return home, my child. Be good and kind and I hope to see you soon!' said the uncle and blessed Leela.

Leela saw that her uncle was not going to get out of bed or give her any presents so she quickly said goodbye.

On the way home she came across the stream. The dam had grown bigger and the water was rushing angrily against the banks. Leela looked and saw a lovely silk scarf floating on the water. 'Ah, there is my present!' she said and jumped into the water. The dam broke and swept Leela with its angry water. Leela tried to catch the scarf but it floated past her. She was thrown against the rocks and hurt her legs very badly. Leela came out of the water limping sadly. She saw the scarf floating down the river but there was nothing she could do to reach it.

By now Leela was very tired. She wanted to sit down and rest for a while. As she sat down, great clouds of smoke came up through the forest. She began to cough and sneeze. She was very frightened. She knew that there was a fire somewhere, burning very angrily.

She saw the fire approaching and ran towards her home. She stumbled on the twigs and fell over the rocks. She brushed against thorny bushes and hit her head against the branches of the trees.

At last she saw her house. She cried out, 'Please help me, please help me!'

Lula was in the house and came rushing out. She saw Leela who was crying and screaming. Her hair was in a mess. Her clothes were torn and her arms and legs were bleeding. 'What happened to you?' asked Lula.

Then Leela told her the story. Lula hugged her sister and whispered, 'Remember what Mama said. Always be good and kind, then kindness will be returned to you.'

5

WISHES COME TRUE

A long time ago in a distant land there lived two rich men. One was kind-hearted and good. He always helped the poor and gave food and money to people who needed it. The other man was a miser who would not help anyone. He was hated and feared by everyone. People made fun of him behind his back saying, 'He is so rich but he helps no one. He is so rich but he cannot do anything about his flat, fat nose.'

As the days went by, the miser became richer and the good man became poor. Until one day the good man found he had no money left at all. He went to his friend the miser and asked if he could borrow some money. The miser refused to help him and said, 'My friend, I knew one day you would lose all your money and wealth. You were always giving your money to poor people. I knew one day you would not have any left for yourself.'

The good man said, 'When I had money I enjoyed sharing it with others. If you let me borrow some money I will give it back to you in a few days.'

The miser laughed and replied, 'I cannot lend you any money because you will only give it away. If you wish you and your wife can work in my house as my servants.'

The good man sighed and said, 'Well, since you will not help me there is nothing else I can do. My wife and I shall work as your servants.'

The miser was a hard master and treated his servants like slaves. He made them do everything and he did nothing for himself. If he wanted a glass of water he shouted for the servant. If he wanted his shoes he would call one of his servants to bring them. The good man and his wife had to work hard for their new master.

One night, after the good man had done his hard day's work, he went to his little room. He washed and cleaned up. Just as he was preparing to eat his simple dinner he heard a knock on the door. He opened the door and saw an old man standing there.

The old man said, 'My friend, I am very tired and I have travelled a long distance. I have lost my way. Will you give me food and shelter for the night?'

The good man said, 'Come in, my friend. You see I am a poor man. I have just taken out my dinner. There is one bowl of rice—let us share it. I am sorry I have nothing else to give you.'

After they had eaten their meal the two men went to sleep.

Early the next morning when the good man woke up he found that the old man had gone. He looked around the room and found a small black box lying in the corner. There was a letter lying on the box. The good man read the letter; it said, 'My friend, peace be with you! I have received great kindness from you. Though you had little to eat you shared it all with me. The box I leave you is a magic box.

32

If you hold it in your hand, close your eyes and make only three wishes they will all come true.'

The good man woke up his wife and told her the exciting news about the magic box.

Then he held the magic box in his hands, closed his eyes and said, 'My first wish is that my wife, who is not keeping well, should get well again.'

The good man opened his eyes and to his surprise and joy he saw that his wife looked well again.

He then made his second wish, 'I wish to have my old grand house back with all its wealth.'

The good man opened his eyes and looked out of the window and saw the house that he had wished for. His house was there, his money was there and all the things he loved were inside the house.

The good man then closed his eyes and said, 'I have everything I want. My third and final wish is this. I never want to be foolish again.'

The good man and his wife were very happy and they went to live in their new home with all their old wealth and riches.

Later that day, the miser came to the good man's house. He asked the good man how he had become rich again. The good man, being truthful, told him all that had happened. Then the miser asked the good man, 'My friend, do you think that you could let me borrow the black box for some time?'

The good man did not say anything. He picked up the magic box and gave it to the miser.

The miser took the box and ran home happily. He sat and thought about the three wishes he would make. He had one great sorrow in his life and that was his flat, fat nose. So he thought to himself that his first wish would be to change his flat, fat nose. The second wish would be to get more money. The third wish would be for a long life so that he could make even more money.

He took the magic box in his hands, closed his eyes and said, 'Oh, magic box, I wish my flat, fat nose would disappear and in its place to have a long, thin nose.' He opened his eyes and ran to the mirror. He looked at his face and saw that he now had a very long, thin nose. When he went outside everyone who saw him started to laugh. 'Have you ever seen a man with such a long, thin nose?' they asked. 'His nose is so long that it dances in front of him! Have you ever seen a man with such a long, lean nose?'

The man rushed back into his house and picked up the magic box and closed his eyes quickly. He cried, 'Magic box, I don't want this long, thin nose.' He opened his eyes and ran to the mirror. What do you think he saw?

He looked at his face in the mirror and found that he had no nose at all!

He went outside and on the road everyone looked at him and laughed. They said, 'Have you ever seen a man with no nose at all? Here comes the funny man with no nose at all!'

The miser rushed home weeping. He picked up the magic box and closed his eyes and cried, 'Magic box, give me back my old nose.'

He went to the mirror and looked at his face. His old flat, fat nose was back in its place.

The next day he went back to the good man and returned the magic box. The miser told him the whole story about his nose. He told him how all three wishes had been wasted on getting his old nose back again. Then he asked the good man what he should do to get the other wishes that he wanted. He wanted to be richer and to live long so that he could make more money. The good man told the wise man what to do. He said:

'Never waste your wishes on the shape of your nose.
Give what you have, your heart must never close.
You will be happy only when you give,
A happy man lives long.
So long may you live.'

35

6

THE JUST KING

Not so long ago there lived four farmers. Each farmer owned a small piece of land. They worked hard from morning till night. Each one looked after his own land. They ploughed the fields and harvested the crop. They had just enough food to feed their family.

Near the village, where the farmers lived, was a lovely large piece of land. There were shrubs and trees on the land. The four farmers often looked at the land and talked amongst themselves. They agreed that if they jointly bought the land and grew cotton on it and sold their cotton then all four of them would make a little bit of money. They all wanted to have a little more money to buy nice clothes for their families.

The four farmers talked about the land for some time. Some years later they were able to buy it. The four of them worked very hard to clear the land. Then they planted cotton plants and soon the cotton buds began to appear. The four farmers looked at the cotton plants and knew that they were going to have a good crop of cotton and make the money that they had been dreaming about. They decided that it would be wise to buy a dog to watch over their new cotton farm. They were afraid that a thief might come and steal their young cotton buds.

The four farmers went in search of a dog. They found a. handsome brown dog. It was clever and as brave as it was good to look at. The four farmers decided that since the farm belonged to all four of them, the dog should also belong to them all. Each farmer paid his share of the money for the dog. On the way home they played with it. One farmer said jokingly, 'This dog belongs to all of us. I own the right front leg of this dog.'

The other farmer friends laughed and said, 'If you own the right front leg of the dog then who owns the left front leg and the back legs?' Each farmer claimed one leg of the dog and went laughing all the way home. The dog was very clever and hard-working and the four farmers were very happy and loved it very much.

As the days went by the cotton buds began to burst and lovely soft white cotton puffs appeared on every plant. The farmers worked hard to pick the cotton carefully. They gathered it in a huge heap in the farmyard. When their work was done they fed their dog and left him to guard the cotton.

One night, a gang of robbers arrived at the village. They prowled around looking for things to steal. One of the robbers saw the huge heap of cotton lying in the corner of the farmyard and told the others about it. They came to steal the cotton in the middle of the night. As the robbers entered the farmyard the dog began to bark and chased them round and round the yard. The robbers ran for their lives. One of them picked up a stone and threw it at the dog and ran away. The stone hit the dog's right front leg very hard.

The next morning the four farmers came to work. When they saw the farmyard in a mess they knew that robbers had paid them a visit. They looked around the yard and saw that nothing had been stolen. They called their dog. From out of the corner came the little limping dog. They all petted and hugged it. They knew that the brave dog had saved their cotton and their wealth.

One of them said, 'Friend, who owns the right front leg of the dog? It is your duty to look after the dog since it is your leg of the dog that is so badly hurt.'

The farmer replied, 'I will certainly look after the dog and bandage his right front leg. But remember that the poor dog hurt his right front leg when he was trying to save the cotton that belongs to all of us.'

Saying this, he took a piece of cloth and soaking it with medicine he bandaged the dog's foot. That day he could not run very fast. The dog's right front leg was so painful that he could not put it down on the ground. The dog spent the morning limping about on three legs.

At lunchtime the four farmer friends stopped working. They lit a fire and heated their food and sat down to eat together. As they were eating and talking, the little dog came sniffing by. He smelt the food and thought he might get an extra bite. Each of the farmers petted the dog and gave him a bit of bread. The dog went wagging its tail from one farmer to the other.

By mistake the dog went too close to the fire. A tiny spark fell on the dog's cloth bandage and caught fire. The fire on his foot frightened him. He went running wildly here and there limping on three feet, howling in pain. The dog ran into the farmyard and brushed past the huge heap of cotton. The cotton heap began to burn and suddenly became a huge heap of fire. Soon there was nothing left but ash.

Meanwhile, the dog ran out into the field and jumped into a nearby pond. He lay in the water for some time catching his breath and soothing his wounded foot.

The four farmers looked at the burnt heap of cotton and cried. They were so angry that they started quarrelling with each other. 'It is your fault!' 'No it is your fault!' they screamed at each other. They knew that their dreams of selling the cotton and making money were all lost. All their hard work of the past several months had all gone up in smoke. Then one farmer said, 'It is the fault of the dog. The man who owns the dog's right front leg is to blame. Because of that foot and the bandage on that foot all our cotton is lost, all our dreams are lost.'

Another farmer said, 'Yes, it is the fault of the right front leg of the dog and its owner. Now you must pay us for all that we have lost.'

The man who owned the right front leg of the dog cried, 'But the dog belongs to all of us. I think it would be fair that we should all share the loss.'

The other three were very angry and said, 'You own the leg that has caused this loss. If you do not pay us for all that we have lost then we will report you to the king.'

The poor farmer worried all night about his bad luck. In the morning the three farmers came to take him to the king. All the way to the king's court the poor farmer cried and cried and said, 'It is not my fault! It is not my fault!'

When they reached the king's court they waited for their turn to meet him. The king listened to the problems that the people had and gave them his advice and told them what to do. Then came the farmers' turn. The king saw three farmers holding on tight to one poor man who was screaming and crying.

The king said, 'What is the matter with this man?'

The three farmers bowed low before the king and told him their story. They told him how they had bought the land together, how they had bought the dog to protect the land and then described how they had lost all their cotton. The king listened to their story.

The king said, 'I see you have decided that the cotton was lost because of the man who owned the right front leg of the dog.'

'Yes, Your Majesty!' replied the three farmers.

On hearing this the king thought for a while. Then he said, 'Now tell me, was the leg so badly hurt that the dog was limping and could not walk on his right front leg?'

The farmers replied, 'Yes, Your Majesty, the dog's right front leg was so badly hurt that the dog could not put it down on the ground. The dog was limping all day long on three legs.'

'This being so,' said the king, 'the dog used only its three good legs while it was running and when the cotton caught fire. The dog was not using his hurt leg when he was running and when the cotton caught fire. Then it was because of the dog's three good legs that the cotton caught fire. I therefore order the three of you to pay the man who owns the hurt right front leg his share of the lost cotton.'

Everyone in the court was amazed at the king's wisdom.

The farmers went home and on the way they became friends again.

They laughed and said, 'How stupid we are! Who can own one leg of a dog? If you love a dog, you must love all of it!'

7

THE WISE OLD MAN

There was a wise old man who lived in a far-away
village. People came to him every day for help and
advice. As he was good and kind, the people were
fond of him. In return for his help and advice the
wise old man asked for nothing.

44

He lived alone and did all the household work himself. He would go to the forest and gather wild fruits to eat. While he was in the forest he would watch the animals and birds. Over the years he learnt many things about the animals and birds of the forest.

Many miles away there was a great city. In the city there lived a great and brave king. The king had fought many battles and had ruled for a long time. He had a favourite camel on which he would ride to battle.

As the years went by, the camel grew old and weak and feeble. The king still loved the camel. The camel was not given any work to do but was allowed to roam about and graze wherever it wanted. In the evening, the camel would come back to its stable and rest for the night.

One day, the camel roamed far away and deep into the forest. It did not return to its stable that evening. The camel-keeper was worried. He searched all night for the king's favourite camel.

In the morning, he had still not been able to find the camel. He returned to the city palace and went to tell the king. He was trembling in fear for he knew that the king's favourite camel was lost.

The king was very sad when he heard the bad news about his camel. He offered a bag of gold to anyone who could find it. Many people went in search of the camel. Many hoped that they would get the bag of gold. No trace of the camel was found anywhere in the kingdom.

Finally, the king sent his soldiers into the forest to find the camel. There the soldiers saw the wise old man sleeping in the shade of a tree. They woke him up and asked him if he had seen the king's camel.

'No,' said the wise old man, 'but tell me, was the camel blind in one eye? Was it lame in one foot? Were some of its teeth missing?'

'You old liar!' said one soldier.

'You have seen the camel!' said another.

'How could you describe the camel so well if you had not seen it?' asked the other soldier.

'I am telling the truth. I have not seen the king's camel.'

'You are a cheat!' said the soldier.

'We do not believe you, come with us to the king!' said the soldiers. They put chains on the old wise man and carried him to the city palace to meet the king.

When the king saw the old man in chains he said, 'Why have you put such an old man in chains? What has he done wrong?'

The soldiers explained to the king what had happened. One soldier said, 'Your Majesty, we went in search of your favourite camel. We saw this man sleeping in the shade of a tree. When we asked him if he had seen the camel he said he had not seen it. Then he asked if the camel was blind in one eye, lame in one foot and had lost a few teeth. We are sure he has seen the camel and knows what it looks like.'

The king was surprised that such an old man would tell a lie. He asked the wise old man to tell him the truth.

'Your Majesty,' said the old man, 'I was able to describe the camel because I live near a forest and watch the animals every day. From the marks that they make I can tell what the animal is like.'

'I see,' said the king, 'you seem to be a wise old man. Come, do not be afraid and tell me what marks helped you describe my camel.'

'Your Majesty,' said the wise old man, 'first, from the footprints on the ground, I could see that no other animal but a camel had gone by. One of the four footprints was a little lighter than the others.

I knew then that the camel (which I had not seen) was lame in one foot. The grass and shrubs on the left side of the path had been eaten but the grass on the right side had not been touched. I was sure that the camel was blind in the right eye. As I followed the footprints of the camel, I saw that bits of grass and half-chewed leaves had fallen on the ground. I could tell that these had fallen from the camel's mouth. I realized that the camel must have lost some of its teeth.'

The king was very impressed to hear these wise words of the wise old man. He ordered that the chains be removed and the wise old man set free. The king requested the wise old man to take a horse and help his soldiers find the camel.

In one day the wise old man was able to trace the camel. The camel was standing alone under a tree near a small stream. The wise old man led it back to the king. The king was delighted that his favourite camel had been found. The king gave the wise old man the bag of gold he had promised anyone who found the camel. The wise old man never took anything from anyone. So he did not accept the bag of gold.

The king then asked the wise old man to stay with him in the palace and be his adviser.

A few days later, the king fell ill. He had a bad cold and cough and could hardly speak. The king asked the wise old man what he should do. The wise old man said, 'Do not worry, Your Majesty; it is all for the best.' This answer did not please the king.

Some days later the king was sharpening his dagger. He sneezed and cut his finger. The finger would not heal and the doctor had to cut it off. The king was very sad to lose his finger. He asked the wise old man why such a thing should happen to him. To this the old man replied again, 'Do not worry, Your Majesty; it is all for the best.'

The king was very angry with the wise old man. What a stupid answer to give a king! So the king sent him to prison. When the old man heard that he was being put into prison he said, 'Do not worry; it is all for the best.'

The king used to go hunting every day. One day while he was out on a hunt his horse got frightened and bolted. The king was thrown off his horse and left all alone in the forest. He got up from the ground and dusted himself clean. Suddenly he heard the roar of a lion. He looked up and the lion was coming towards him.

As a child the king had learnt that a lion would never touch a dead man. So he quickly lay down and pretended he was dead. The lion came near the king. He sniffed the king's clothes. He saw the king's missing finger. The lion thought that the king was dead and went on his way.

It was already dark when the king returned to his palace. His family was very happy to see the king and that he was safe. While the king was resting he began to think of the wise old man in prison. He asked his soldiers to bring the wise old man to see him.

The king said, 'I see that you were right when you told me that it is all for the best that I lost my finger.'

'Thank you, Your Majesty!' replied the wise old man.

Then the king asked him, 'While it may have been right for me to lose a finger, why did you say that it was all for the best when I put you in prison?'

'Your Majesty,' replied the wise old man, 'had I not gone to prison, I would have gone with you on the hunt. I would have been by your side. I would also have lain down on the ground when the lion appeared. I would have pretended to be dead. The lion thought you were dead and wounded since one of your fingers was missing. Then the lion would have most certainly killed me. So, Your Majesty, it was all for the best that I was thrown into prison.'

The king was very happy to hear the clever reply. He said to the wise old man, 'You are really clever. Stay with me and from now on I will listen to what you have to say, even though it may not always please me.'

The wise old man winked and said, 'Do not worry, Your Majesty; it is all for the best!'

8

TWICE BLESSED

Two men were travelling on the same road. One was a poor, honest weaver who never dreamt of doing any wrong. The other was a lazy fellow, who had never done an honest day's work in his life. All he did was to travel from place to place robbing people whom he met.

52

Both men were walking and began to talk. It was hot and they soon got tired. The men stopped by a roadside well to drink water. Having drunk their fill of good, clean water, they lay down in the shade and rested for a while. While they were resting, another traveller stopped at the well to drink water. He came near the well and put down the bundle that he was carrying. He picked up the bucket to fetch some water. The lazy fellow crept up behind the traveller and was going to push him into the well and run away with his bundle. The good weaver saw what was happening and rushed and saved the traveller. The lazy fellow quickly ran away.

Soon after the weaver began his journey again. Along the way he met the lazy fellow once again. The lazy fellow said, 'A curse be upon you for stopping me. I could have robbed that traveller's bundle.'

The weaver said nothing and walked on quietly. They had hardly walked a few steps when the lazy fellow struck his foot against something and cried out. When they looked down they saw that he had hit his toe against a large purse which was full of money. 'Truly this is luck!' cried the lazy fellow and ran off with the money. The weaver could do nothing.

The weaver went on his way alone. A little while later as he was walking he stepped on a thorn. The sharp point pierced his foot and he cried out in pain, 'What a cruel fate is mine! Here I am always trying to be good. In return for this I suffer and that lazy fellow becomes rich. Allah is most unjust and unfair. I get a thorn and the lazy fellow gets a purse full of money. How can I believe that God is fair and just?'

Crying with pain, he pulled the thorn out of his foot. When he looked up he saw a grand old man with a long, flowing white beard. 'What makes you so unhappy, my friend?' asked the grand old man.

The weaver told him his story and said 'Am I not right in saying that Allah is not just and fair?'

'I am sorry. I do not agree with you. I have seen good and bad men. But Allah is always fair and just.'

'I beg you, ask Allah why money is thrown in front of a lazy man and why a thorn was put in my path to hurt me?'

The grand old man said, 'There is a reason. Look at me! I am a fakir. I pray without fail five times a day. When I beg for alms, I call out His name. I get scraps of food while others who say no prayers at all eat and drink in plenty.'

The fakir and the weaver continued on their travels. They soon came to a well and stopped to drink some water and rest. As they were sitting beneath a shady tree they saw a large poisonous snake go by. The fakir shook his head and started to laugh. 'I know why a thorn was lying in your path.'

'Why?' asked the weaver.

'Perhaps as the thorn went into your foot, a poisonous snake was passing by. You lifted your foot and cried out in pain. The poisonous snake slipped by. The thorn, though painful, may have saved your life.'

'While that may be true about me, what about the lazy fellow who struck his foot against the purse full of money?'

The fakir pointed to a huge anthill beside the tree and said, 'You see the anthill? Look how hard the clever ants are working to build it. That lazy fellow is also a clever fellow. If he worked hard he could be a very rich man. Instead he is a common thief who lives each day by what he can steal from others.'

'While you may be right about me and the lazy fellow, why are you so poor though you are so good?'

The fakir did not have an answer to that.

The weaver and the fakir continued on their journey. As night began to fall, they stopped and looked for a place to rest. It was an old empty house near the road. They went inside and began to clean it up. While the weaver was sweeping the floor he found in the heap of mud a gold coin. 'Look what I have found!' he cried with joy. The fakir was happy for his friend and made his bed to sleep. The weaver thought for a while and said to the grand old fakir, 'You are so kind and good I want to give you this coin.'

The fakir thanked the weaver for his kindness, and put the gold coin under his pillow. Then he said his prayers and went to sleep. The next morning when the sun began to rise in the eastern sky the two men woke up. In the darkness they saw that there were two gold coins, instead of one, under the pillow. So each one got a gold coin.

The fakir was very happy. He was filled with joy and took his gold coin to the market. There he bought sweets and fruit and all the things that he had not enjoyed for so many years. He brought them all back to the hut and shared them with his friend. But there were still lots of sweets and fruits left over. Then he said his prayers and thanked Allah for all the good things he had been given.

As the two friends were about to go to sleep, there was a gentle knock on the door. Opening it they found two beggars begging for alms.

The fakir said, 'Money I do not have but we have lots of food to eat. In the name of Allah the merciful you are welcome to eat.'

The two beggars ate their fill and thanked the fakir and went away.

The weaver was watching everything and said, 'I know now why you have no money. Though your wants are few, whatever you have you give to others. Even if you had money you would always be poor.'

'Poor and happy!' said the fakir. 'If I had lots of money you would see how I enjoyed myself and how much I was able to save.'

The fakir said his prayers and went to sleep. The next morning the two men woke up and lo! The fakir found another gold coin under his pillow. He said his prayers and went rushing to the market. Once again he bought lots of sweets and fruit. After eating as much as he could he brought the rest home.

After he had said his prayers, he went to sleep. Late at night he heard a gentle knock. This time it was two pilgrims requesting him for some money. 'Money I do not have but please come in. In the name of Allah, share the sweets and food that I have,' said the fakir.

Now to his joy and happiness, the same thing happened every morning. The fakir found a gold coin under his pillow.

After a week, the fakir asked the weaver, 'Why is Allah so good and kind to me? I was given money once and with it I bought all the things I liked. Why does Allah give me good things every day?'

'Well,' said the weaver, 'I have been watching you all this week. At the beginning of the week you were complaining that you had no money. You prayed every day and were still able to collect scraps. When you got the gold coin what did you do? You bought sweets and fruits and in the name of Allah you shared it with your friend and even with strangers. Do you not know that he who gives joyfully in the name of Allah is twice blessed?'

The fakir was overjoyed to hear this and promised that he would never complain again. Then he asked, 'You are also a poor and a good man. What have you received?'

The weaver replied, 'I got a thorn in my foot that may have saved me from a snake. I found a friend who has taught me how to live. I too am twice blessed!'

9

YOUR LAST CHANCE

This is a story about a very rich merchant who had a very foolish son. The merchant was sad, for though he was very rich he was sure that his son would lose all his wealth.

The wealthy merchant died and the son was left alone to look after his father's riches. Being foolish, the boy lost all his wealth and had no money left to buy clothes and food for himself.

One day, he was sitting under a tree and crying when an old man saw him. The old man stopped and asked him, 'My boy, why are you crying?'

The boy said, 'Old man, when my father died he left me a lot of money. But I was foolish and I have lost it all and now I am starving.'

'I am very sorry to hear that, my boy,' said the old man. 'I can help you if you like. Can you see the mountains far away in the distance? Beyond the mountains and over the seas lives Mr Luck. Tell him your story and I am sure he will give you back your luck.'

'Thank you very much!' said the boy, 'I will do as you say.'

The boy packed a few clothes and his things in a bundle and set off on his journey to find Mr Luck.

He travelled for many days. He climbed hills and crossed great rivers. He slept under the stars and walked in the hot sun. Then he came to a deep, dark forest. As he was walking through the forest he saw a huge lion standing right in the middle of his path. The boy trembled with fear and thought that this was the end.

The boy looked at the lion carefully. He soon realized that the lion was not so frightening after all. In fact, the lion was old and unable to run. The lion turned to the boy and said, 'You look weary and tired. You look as though you are going on a long journey. Where are you going?'

The boy told the lion his troubles and added that he was on his way to find Mr Luck.

'Hurrah!' said the lion, 'I shall not kill you if you do something for me.'

'Yes, sir,' said the boy, 'tell me what it is you want me to do, and I shall do it.'

'Good,' said the lion 'when you meet Mr Luck, tell him that I have become very old and cannot run fast and hunt as I used to. Ask him what I should do to become strong again.'

'Sure,' said the boy. In order not to forget, he tied a knot on a string that he was carrying and went his way.

After travelling for a few days he came to a lake. There he saw a very strange sight. A huge fish was rolling around in the shallow water. 'Hello!' said the boy, 'What is the matter with you? Why are you rolling about in the shallow water when you can swim in the deep?'

'That is easier said than done!' replied the fish. 'Alas! I have a bad pain in my stomach. It makes me roll around in pain. I cannot swim into the deep water any longer.'

'Tell me,' continued the fish, 'where are you going?'

The boy told the fish all his troubles and said, 'I am going to find Mr Luck and to ask for his help.'

'Ah!' said the fish, 'Will you tell Mr Luck my troubles too and ask him what I should do?'

'Sure,' said the boy and so saying, he tied another knot on his string and went on his journey.

After many days he came to the bank of a magnificent river. There were thousands of people working near the river to build the wall of a big dam. They were building the dam to store water to use in their fields. He looked and saw that the king was sitting underneath a big silk umbrella watching the people building the dam across the river. He did not look very happy. The boy went up to the king and bowing his head told him where he was going.

Then the boy asked the king why he was looking so sad. The king shook his head and replied, 'You see, my boy, I am unhappy because each time we build this dam the rain and floods come and wash the wall away. When you find Mr Luck will you ask him what I should do?'

'Yes, Your Majesty, I certainly will!' said the boy.

The boy tied another knot on his string and went on. After a few days, he came to a huge palace. He looked in and saw a lovely princess sitting in the garden. The boy asked the guard of the palace to give him permission to talk to the princess.

He went into the garden and said to her, 'Your Majesty, I am on my way to find Mr Luck. I was going past your palace and I saw you looking very sad and sitting alone in the garden. What is the matter?'

The princess said, 'I am sad. Very sad. I am a princess. This huge palace is mine. But I am sad. If you find Mr Luck please ask him what I should do to be happy?'

'Sure, Princess, I shall be happy to ask him,' said the boy. He tied another knot on his string and went on.

After a few days, the boy met a beautiful black horse with a very nice saddle on his back. The horse was standing all by itself with no one to ride him. The boy patted the horse on his neck and told ' horse his sad story and where he was go' horse said, 'Please, sir, when you meet Mr Luck tell him I am very lonely and sad. I have this lovely saddle on my back and do not know what to do with it.'

The boy promised to do so and tied the fifth knot on the string.

After days of travelling he came to the high mountains. He climbed the mountains and found a huge cave. He entered the cave and found an old man with a long, white beard sitting all alone.

The boy thought that this had to be Mr Luck. He went close to the old man and said, 'Wise sir, tell me, are you Mr Luck? I have travelled many days and nights to find you.'

The old man smiled and said, 'Well, my boy, tell me what it is you want. What can I do for you?'

The boy told him how he had lost all the money that his father had left for him. Then the old man said, 'I see you have been very foolish. Hereafter, you must work hard. Remember this:

If you get a chance,
Do not miss that chance.
Take it, at once,
to ह *Or else, you will remain a dunce!'*

hanked the wise old man and was about
remembered his string with the

five knots. He turned to the old man and said, 'Wise sir, on my travels I met several others. Each one told me their problem and asked me to ask you what they should do.'

The boy then sat and told the wise old man all the stories. The wise old man told the boy what he should tell each of his friends.

The boy thanked the wise old man and started on his homeward journey. On the way he met the horse, the princess, then the king and the fish. At last he came to the deep, dark forest and there he met the lion who was waiting for him.

Seeing the boy, the lion said, 'Ah! I see you have returned. Did you meet Mr Luck and did he tell you how to get back your wealth and riches? I hope you asked him about me also?'

'Yes,' said the boy, 'I asked him about you and about four other friends I met along the way. Each one had a problem and Mr Luck told me what to tell them.'

'How interesting!' said the lion. 'Come and sit in the shade of the tree and tell me the story of each of your friends and what Mr Luck told them to do.'

'Well,' said the boy, 'Mr Luck said to me:

> *If you get a chance,*
> *Do not lose that chance.*
> *Take it, at once.*
> *Or else, you will remain a dunce.'*

'How interesting!' said the lion.

'Then he told me to tell the sad and lonely horse to find somebody to ride him.'

'What did the horse say when you told him this?' asked the lion.

'When I told the horse he asked me to get on to the nice saddle and ride him.'

'Well? What did you say to the horse?' asked the lion.

The boy replied, 'Oh, horse, you are too fine to ride.'

'Rrr, Rrr!' sighed the lion. 'You missed your chance, you silly dunce!'

Then the boy said, 'I met the sad and lonely princess in the lovely palace. I told her that Mr Luck had said that she should find some nice young man to marry.'

'Well,' asked the lion, 'when you told the princess this what did she say?'

'The princess asked me to marry her. She asked me if I would like to live in the lovely palace and be her husband.'

'What did you tell her?' asked the lion.

'I told her I could not marry a princess because I was such a poor boy.'

'Rrr, Rrr, Rrr!' groaned the lion. 'You lost another chance, you silly dunce!'

'I went to the king who was building the dam that was always falling down. I told him that Mr Luck had said that the king should stop building the dam across the river and to make lakes and ponds to collect water instead. Mr Luck advised him to give half his kingdom to anyone who really helped him. The king asked if I wanted half his kingdom.'

'Well? What did you say to the king?' asked the lion.

'I told the king that I was not fit to be a king as I am just a foolish boy.'

The lion roared loudly, 'Rrr, Rrr, Rrr, Rrr! Once, twice, three times! You lost your chance. You very silly dunce.'

Then the boy said, 'I went to see the fish with the stomach-ache. I told him what Mr Luck had said that he was in pain because he had swallowed a box of jewels. If someone could press the fish's stomach then the box would come out.'

'Well? What happened?' asked the lion getting a little impatient.

'The fish asked me to press his stomach. Out came the box of jewels and the fish was able to swim again. The fish thanked me and presented me with the box of jewels.'

'Well?' asked the lion.

'I told the fish that I did not know what to do with such costly jewels.'

'Rrr, Rrr, Rrr, Rrr, Rrr!, growled the lion,

'If you get a chance,
Do not lose that chance.
Take it, at once.
Or else, you remain a dunce!'

'Last,' said the boy, 'I told Mr Luck that you were sad, old and unable to run. He told me to tell you this secret. You should find a dunce and eat his right hand. Then you will grow strong again.'

The lion roared and laughed at the same time, 'Rrr, Rrr! Ha Ha! Rrr, Rrr, Ha Ha! Rrr, Rrr! This was your last chance! I do not think I have ever met someone as foolish as you. I do not think I ever *want* to meet someone as foolish as you.'

With one small jump he sprang on the boy and bit his hand off.

10

REAL FRIENDS

In a forest there lived a jackal. He had made a hole to live in near a tall peepal tree. On that tree lived a pretty, soft-spoken dove. Lots of other birds loved to visit the peepal tree because there were always fruits and insects to eat. The jackal and the dove soon became friends. They spent a lot of time talking to each other and playing about in the leaves and plants near the tree. They talked about what was happening in the tree and what was happening in the sky. The dove always had to be a little careful because the jackal was much bigger than her and she did not like to get too close.

One day, the jackal said to the dove, 'You say that you are my friend, but are you really my friend? A friend is someone who can make you laugh, make you cry and someone who will save your life if need be. You little dove cannot make me laugh nor can you make me cry. I am sure that if I were in danger you would not be able to save my life. So tell me, are you my real friend?'

The dove could not do very much so she said to the jackal, 'Friends also like to talk to each other, they like to spend time playing with each other. So let us be friends. Let us talk to each other, let us spend time with each other. Maybe when the time is right, I will be able to show you that I am also a really good friend.'

A few days later, two people were passing by. One was a very fat, fashionable lady wearing strange party clothes and the other was her husband who was looking very sad. The fat lady walked a few steps and cried, 'Stop! You are walking too fast. My shoes hurt and my dress will get spoilt.' The poor husband walked a little slower but said nothing.

A few steps later, the fat lady screamed, 'Stop! Do not walk so fast. My dress is getting dirty. Do I look all right?'

The husband said nothing but walked on slowly.

The jackal was sitting near the tree and watching the husband and wife walking by. He laughed at the sight of this funny couple.

The dove was in the tree, busy cleaning her little nest.

Suddenly, the fat lady screamed, 'STOP! STOP! Look what that stupid bird has done right on my nice, new dress! My dress is spoilt and my hair is dirty. Oh dear! Oh dear!'

The jackal saw what had happened and began to laugh.

As the fat lady was cleaning her dress, she became angrier and angrier. Her face became red and sweaty. She was huffing, panting and she looked more and more terrible. 'Do I look all right? Do I look all right?' she screamed at her husband.

'No, dear, you look terrible!' said the husband.

Hearing this the fat lady rushed at her husband and hit him. He started to run and the fat lady ran after him.

71

The jackal who was watching all this, began to laugh so much that he thought he would burst his sides.

Hearing the jackal laugh, the little dove said, 'Now do you believe that I can make you laugh? Now do you believe that I am a real friend?'

'Yes, yes,' said the jackal unable to stop his laughter. 'But you, little dove, cannot make me cry!'

A few days later, the two friends saw a hunter with his hunting dogs coming into the forest. The jackal quickly ran into his hole to hide and the dove flew into the tree.

When the hunter came a little closer, the dove flew past them and fell to the ground near them. She began to hop about as if she had hurt herself. Seeing that there was something wrong with the dove, the hunting dogs came nearer. The dove began to run and the dogs followed. She then quickly flew into the tree. But the dogs were no longer interested in the dove as they had smelt the jackal in the hollow near the tree. The dogs began to bark and snarl for they could smell the jackal. The jackal was trembling inside his hole. He knew he could not come out till the dogs went away. The jackal was so frightened that he began to cry. He called out for help.

Soon the dogs got tired of waiting for the jackal to come out and went running off to look for their master.

The jackal came out of his hole feeling sore, stiff and miserable. His eyes were red and the tears were still rolling down his cheeks. The dove looked down from above and said, 'Did you have a good cry?'

The jackal was very angry and snapped, 'Keep quiet! You saw how those dogs behaved. They could have killed me.'

A few days later, when the two friends were talking again, the jackal said, 'I know that you can make me laugh and you can make me cry. But are you a real friend? Will you save my life if I am in danger?'

The dove said nothing.

Time passed and the summer days were over. The leaves on the trees began to fall. The cold days of winter had begun. During the evening and most of the night, the jackal went out hunting. Food for the jackal was becoming difficult to find. He began to go further and further away from the tree and the little dove, in search of food.

One evening, the jackal returned to the tree and looked for the dove. She was nowhere to be seen. He waited below the tree to meet her before going to sleep. The jackal soon got tired of waiting and decided to go into his hole near the tree.

Just then, the jackal heard the rustling of wings and the shrill screech of a bird. He pulled his nose out of the hole and looked up. There was the little dove, flapping her wings and screeching, 'Do not go in! Do not go in!'

The jackal ran away from his hole and sat at a distance.

'What is the matter?' asked the jackal.

'Thank goodness! I caught you just in time. While you were away, a young python came by and has occupied your hole near the tree. Had you gone any further, he would most certainly have eaten you up. I saw him the other day eating a whole deer, head, feet, bones and all!'

After a little while, the jackal got over his fright. He stopped panting and could speak again. 'Thank you! You saved my life! Now I believe that you are a real friend of mine.'

The dove looked down from the tree and said, 'A good friend is one who asks for nothing, always ready to do something. I may be a good friend, of yours, jackal. But are you a good friend of mine?'